Adapted by Mary Tillworth

Based on the teleplay "Triple-Track Train Race" by Robert Scull

Illustrated by Eren Unten

 A GOLDEN BOOK • NEW YORK

T#: 306093
randomhousekids.com
ISBN 978-0-553-49769-4
Printed in the United States of America
10 9 8 7 6 5 4 3 2 1

Molly and Gil were swimming to school one morning when they heard a loud whistle.

"Let's go check it out!" said Gil. The two Guppies followed the sound to a busy train station.

As a passenger train pulled away from the station, Gil and Molly spotted someone fixing the whistle on a small black train.

"There's the engineer who works on the train!" said Molly.

The engineer smiled. "This here's Ol' Number Nine. She's a steam locomotive—and she's over a hundred years old!" He patted the whistle. "Ol' Number Nine is gonna need this if she's gonna be in the Triple-Track Train Race today!"

When Gil and Molly got to school, they told all their friends about Ol' Number Nine.

"When the engineer blew the whistle, it went *woo-woo*!" said Gil.

"What does *engineer* mean?" asked Oona.

"The engineer is the person who drives the train," explained Nonny.

"Let's think about trains," said Mr. Grouper.
"Trains get from here to there by riding along . . ."
"Tracks!" said Molly.

Mr. Grouper nodded.
"And trains stop and pick
people up at the . . ."
"Station!" said Goby.

The Bubble Guppies chugged off to lunch in engineer
costumes.

"What did you get for lunch, Nonny?" asked Oona.

Nonny opened his lunch box. "*Track*-eroni and cheese!"

Later that day, Mr. Grouper told the Guppies he was taking them to the Triple-Track Train Race.

"Field trip!" they cheered excitedly. They couldn't wait to watch Ol' Number Nine race against the *Superliner* passenger train and the *Mighty Miss* freight train!

Molly, Gil, and Bubble Puppy joined the engineer in Ol' Number Nine. The three trains lined up at the starting gate.

"Ladies and gentlemen, start your engines!" called the announcer.

A checkered flag dropped—and the trains were off!

The trains were neck and neck when they
went around the first corner. But then the
Superliner pulled in front.
"Wow, that's a really fast train!" said Gil.

Molly and Gil saw a steep mountain up ahead. One track went around it, another track went over it, and a third track went through it.

The Superliner reached the mountain first.

"Ladies and gentlemen, the Superliner is going around the mountain!" called the announcer.

The Mighty Miss roared up to the mountain and took the track that went over it.

Whistling and tooting, Ol' Number Nine took the track through the mountain.

"In just a few moments, we should be able to see the trains as they come around to the finish line," said the announcer.

In the distance, a whistle blew. Ol' Number Nine came chugging out of the tunnel. She was in first place!

The engineer blew the whistle again. He didn't see
the whistle come loose and tumble off the train!
    Just then, a herd of cows stepped onto the tracks.
    "Look out!" cried Molly.
    The engineer pulled the brakes, and Ol' Number
Nine screeched to a halt.

"Quick, Molly, pull the whistle!"
said Gil.
   But when Molly pulled, there was
no sound.

"Oh, no! We lost our whistle!" said the engineer.

Molly and Gil could hear the other trains approaching behind them. "What are we going to do?" asked Molly.

Bubble Puppy leapt out and ran down the track. He picked up the train whistle and took it to the engineer.

"I'd better put this back on, quick!" said the engineer. He fastened the whistle onto the train.

Molly blew the whistle, and the cows
moved out of the way. "All clear!" she called.
The engineer started the train, and Ol' Number
Nine raced ahead—with the express train and
the freight train right behind!

"This is going to be incredibly close!" shouted the announcer as the trains neared the finish line. Ol' Number Nine whistled and chugged . . . and crossed the line first!

"Thanks, kids," said Ol' Number Nine's engineer.
"I couldn't have done it without you. And a special
thanks to you, Bubble Puppy!"
"*Fin*-tastic!" cheered the Bubble Guppies.